KT-385-272

Mortimer the Raven is causing yet more chaos and mayhem in Rumbury Town. Things get even worse when Arabel takes Mortimer roller-skating with her three nasty cousins Cindy, Mindy and Lindy. But when Arabel gets very ill and is languishing in hospital it is Mortimer who saves her, though some of the other patients have a difficult time – to say nothing of the staff!

OTHER BOOKS BY JOAN AIKEN

Joan Aiken

Mortimer's Bread Bin

ILLUSTRATED BY QUENTIN BLAKE

BARN OWL BOOKS

First published in Great Britain 1974
by the British Broadcasting Corporation
35 Marylebone High Street, London W1M 4AA
This edition first published 2001 by Barn Owl Books,
15 New Cavendish Street, London W1M 7RL
Barn Owl Books are distributed
by Frances Lincoln

Text copyright © 1974, 2001 Joan Aiken
Illustrations copyright © 1974, 2001 Quentin Blake
The moral right of Joan Aiken to be identified as author and
Quentin Blake as illustrator of this work has been asserted

ISBN 1 903015 15 4
A CIP catalogue record for this book
is available from the British Library

Designed and typeset by Douglas Martin
Printed and bound in Great Britain
by Cox & Wyman Limited, Reading

For Elise

Chapter One

All the things I am going to tell you now happened during one terrible, wild, wet week in February, when Mortimer the raven had been living with the Jones family in Rumbury Town, London N.W.3^1/$_2$ for several months. The weather had been so dreadful for so long that everybody in the family was, if not in a bad temper, at least less cheerful than usual.

Mrs Jones complained that even the bread felt damp unless it was made into toast, Arabel had the beginnings of a cold, Mr Jones found it very tiring to drive his taxi through pouring rain along greasy skiddy roads day after day, and Mortimer the raven was annoyed because there were two things he wanted to do, and he was not permitted to do either of them. He wanted to be given a ride round the garden on Arabel's red truck; Mrs Jones would not allow it because of the weather; and he wanted to climb into the bread bin and go to sleep there. It seemed to him highly unreasonable that he was not allowed to do this.

"We could keep the bread somewhere else," Arabel said.

"So I buy a bread bin that costs three pound and eighty-seven pence for a great, black, sulky, lazy bird to sleep in? What's wrong with the coal scuttle? He's slept in that for the last three weeks. So it's suddenly not comfortable any more?"

Mrs Jones had just come back from shopping, very wet; she began taking groceries and vegetables out of her wheeled shopping-bag and dumping them on the kitchen floor. She hung her dripping umbrella beside the tea-towels.

"He wants a change," Arabel said, looking out of the window at the grey lines of rain that went slamming across the garden like telephone wires.

"Oh, naturally! Ginger marmalade on crumpets that bird gets for his breakfast, spaghetti and meat-balls for lunch, brandysnaps for supper, allowed to sit inside the grandfather clock whenever he wants, *and* slide down the stairs whenever he feels like it on my best wedding tray painted with pink and green gladioli, and he must have a change as well? That bird gets more attention that the Lord Mayor of Hyderabad."

"*He* doesn't know that," Arabel said. "He's never been to Hyderabad."

"So we could all do with a change," said Mrs Jones. "What's so particular about him that he should get one when the rest of us have to do without?"

Arabel and Mortimer went slowly away into the front hall. After a while Arabel picked up Mortimer, sat him on one of her roller-skates, tied a bit of string to it, and pulled him around the downstairs part of the house. But neither of them cheered up much. Arabel's throat felt tight and tickly. Mortimer knew all the scenery too well to be interested in the trip. He rode along with his head sunk down between his shoulders and his beak sunk down among his chest feathers, and his back and wing feathers all higgledy-piggledly, as if he didn't care which way they pointed.

The telephone rang.

Mortimer meant to get to it first – he loved answering the telephone – but he had one of his long toenails caught in the roller-skate. Kicking and flapping to free himself he started the skate

rolling, shot through the hall door, across the
kitchen, knocked over Mrs Jones's openwork
vegetable rack, which had four pounds of brussel
sprouts in the top compartment, and cannoned off
that into a bag of coffee beans and a tall container
of oven spray, which began shooting out thick
frothy foam. Mrs Jones's umbrella fell off the
towel-hanger and stabbed clean through a ripe
melon which had rolled underneath. A fierce
white smoke came boiling off the oven-spray

which made everybody cough; Mrs Jones rushed
to open the window. A lot of rain and wind blew
in, knocking over a tall jar of daffodils that stood
on the window-sill; Mortimer, who was interested
in putting rough, knobbly things underneath flat,
smooth things, began quickly sliding the daffodils
(which were made of plastic) underneath the
kitchen mat.

"Don't touch that foam!" said Mrs Jones, and
she grabbed a large handful of paper towels and

mopped it up. The telephone went on ringing.

Mortimer suddenly noticed the open window; he left the daffodils, climbed up the handles of the drawers under the kitchen sink, very fast, claw over claw, scrabbled along the edge of the sink, hoisted himself up on to the sill, and looked out into the wild, wet, windy garden.

"Drat that phone!" said Mrs Jones, mopping up the last of the foam, and rushed to the front hall. Just as she got there, the telephone stopped ringing.

Mortimer, leaning out of the window, saw that Arabel's red truck was down below on the grass, with half an inch of rain inside it. He jumped out.

"Mortimer!" said Arabel. "Come inside! You'll get wet."

Mortimer was wet already. He was loving it. He took no notice of Arabel.

There were half a dozen conkers floating in the red truck. The next door cat, Ginger, was sitting under a holly-bush, trying to keep dry. Mortimer stood in the truck (the water came up to his knee feathers) and began throwing conkers at Ginger.

"Mortimer!" said Arabel, hanging out of the window. "You are not to throw conkers at Ginger.

He's never done you any harm."

Mortimer took no notice. He threw another conker.

Arabel wriggled back off the draining-board, opened the back door, ran out into the wet garden, grabbed the string of the truck, and pulled it back indoors, with Mortimer on board.

A good deal of the water slopped out on to the kitchen floor; it was like a tidal wave carrying the coffee beans and brussels sprouts towards the hall door.

"*Arabel*," said Mrs Jones coming back into the kitchen. "Have you been out of doors in your bedroom slippers? Oh my stars, if you don't catch your mortal end one of these days my name's Mrs Gypsy Petulengro!"

"I had to fetch Mortimer, he was getting wet," said Arabel. "I stayed on the path."

"Getting wet?" Mrs Jones said. "Why shouldn't he get wet? So you think we should dry him off with the hair-dryer? Birds are *meant* to get wet; that's what they have feathers for."

"Kaaaark," said Mortimer. He shook his feathers. Drops of rain flew about the kitchen.

Mrs Jones shoved the truck outside, slammed

the back door, and began to mop the floor, among the sprouts and the coffee-beans.

The phone began to ring again.

Arabel thought the hair-dryer was a good idea. While Mrs Jones hurried off to answer the telephone, Arabel took the hair-dryer out of its

box, plugged it in, and started blowing Mortimer dry. She put her feet one on each side of him to hold him in place and blew them at the same time, as they were rather cold.

All Mortimer's feathers stood on end, making him look like a turkey. He was so startled that he

said, "Nevermore!" and stepped backwards into a pan of bread rolls that Mrs Jones had set to rise in front of the kitchen fire. He sank into the dough up to his ankles and left a trail of footprints across the pan from corner to corner. But he enjoyed being dried and turned round several times so that Arabel could blow him all over.

"That was Auntie Brenda," said Mrs Jones, coming back ofter a long chat. She was in a hurry to finish the mopping and didn't notice Arabel putting away the hair-dryer. "She says she's taking her lot roller-skating at the rink and she'll stop by and pick us up too."

"Oh," said Arabel."

"Don't you want to go roller-skating?" said Mrs Jones.

"Well I expect Mortimer will enjoy it," said Arabel.

"I just hope he doesn't disgrace us," said Mrs Jones, giving Mortimer an old-fashioned look. "But I'm not going out and leaving him alone in the house. Never shall I forget, not if I was to live to eighty and be elected Beauty Queen of the Home Counties, the time we went to Babes in the Wood and when we got back he'd eaten the banisters and the bathroom basin complete and two-and-a-half packets of assorted Rainbow Bath Oil Bubble Gums."

"Nevermore!" said Mortimer.

"Promises, promises," said Mrs Jones.

"The house looked lovely, all full of bubbles," Arabel said. "Mortimer thought so too."

"Anyway he's not having the chance to do it again. Put your coat on. Auntie Brenda will be here in ten minutes."

Arabel put her coat on very slowly. Her throat tickled worse and worse; she did not feel in the least like going out. Also, although they were her cousins, she was not very fond of Brenda's lot. There were three of them: their names were Lindy, Mindy, and Cindy. As a matter of fact, they were horrible girls. They had unkind natures and liked to say things on purpose to hurt other people's feelings. They were always eating, not from hunger but from greed; they thought it was clever to pester their mother into buying them fruit gums and bottles of coke and bags of crisps and choc-ices all the time they were out. They had more toys than they could be bothered to play with. And they had a lot of spots too.

They had not yet met Mortimer.

Aunt Brenda stopped outside the house in her shiny new car.

Cindy, Lindy and Mindy put their heads out of the window and stopped eating chocolate macaroni sticks long enough to scream:

"Hello, Arabel! We've got new coats, new boots, new furry hoods, new furry gloves, new skirts and new roller-skates!"

"Spoilt lot," muttered Mrs Jones, putting Arabel's old roller-skates into her tartan wheeled shopping-bag. "So what was wrong with the other ones, I should like to know? Anyone would think their Dad was president of the Bank of Monte Carlo."

In fact their Dad was a traveller in do-it-yourself wardrobe kits; he travelled so much that he was hardly ever at home.

Arabel went out to the car in her old coat, old hood, old gloves, and old boots. She held Mortimer tightly. He was very interested when he caught sight of the car, his eyes shone like black satin buttons.

"We're going in that car, Mortimer," Arabel told him.

"Kaaaark," said Mortimer.

Lindy and Cindy hung out of the back seat window shouting, "Arabel, Arabel, 'orrible Arabel, 'orrible, 'orrible, 'orrible Arabel."

Then they spotted Mortimer and their eyes went as round as CD discs.

"Coo!" said Lindy. "What's that?"

"What *have* you got there, 'orrible Arabel?" said Cindy.

"He's our raven. His name's Mortimer," said Arabel.

All three girls burst into screams of laughter.

"A *raven*? What d'you want a *raven* for? Anyway he's not a raven – he's just a rusty old rook. He's just a junky old jackdaw. What's the use of him? Can he talk?"

"If he wants to," said Arabel.

Cindy, Lindy and Mindy laughed even louder.

"I bet all he can say is Caw! See-saw, old Jacky Daw. All he can do is croak and caw!"

"Stop teasing, girls, and make room for Arabel in the back," said Auntie Brenda.

Arabel and Mortimer got into the back and sat there without saying anything. Cindy started to give Mortimer's tail feathers a tweak, but he turned his head right round on its rusty black neck and looked at her so fiercely that she changed her mind.

Mrs Jones got into the front beside her sister Brenda and they were off.

Mortimer had never ridden in a car before – at least not when he was conscious. He liked it. As soon as he had made sure that Arabel's cousins were not likely to attack him at once, he began to bounce up and down gently on Arabel's shoulder, looking out at the shops of Rumbury High Street flashing past, at the red buses swishing along, at the street lamps like a string of salmon-coloured daisies, the scarlet letter-boxes and the greengrocers, all red and green and orange and yellow.

"Nevermore," he muttered. "Nevermore, nevermore."

"There you see," said Arabel, "he *can* speak."

"But what does he mean?" giggled Mindy.

"He means that where he comes from they don't have buses and greengrocers and street lamps and letter-boxes."

"I don't believe you know what he means at all."

After that, Arabel kept quiet.

Chapter Two

When they arrived at Rumbury Borough Roller-
skating Rink, Mortimer was even more amazed at
the sign above the entrance, which was picked out
in pink lights. The forecourt was paved with
yellow glass tiles.

"You get the tickets, Martha, I'll put the car in
the car park," said Auntie Brenda.

Arabel's three cousins were all expert roller-
skaters. They came to the rink two or three times
every week. They buckled on their new skates
and shot off into the middle, knocking over any
amount of people on the way.

Arabel, when she had put on her skates, went
slowly and carefully round the edge. She did not
want to risk being knocked into, because
Mortimer was perched on her shoulder.

Also she felt very tired, and her throat had
stopped tickling and was now really sore. And

24

her feet were cold. And her head ached.

Auntie Brenda came back from putting away the car and sat down by Mrs Jones, and the two sisters began talking their heads off.

We'll have to stay here for hours yet, thought Arabel.

"Come on into the middle, cowardy custard! Caw, caw, cowardy cowardy!" screamed Lindy and Cindy.

"Yes, go on, ducky, you'll be all right, there's nothing to be afraid of," called Auntie Brenda. But Arabel shook her head and stuck to the edge.

Mortimer was having a lovely time. He didn't mind Arabel's going slowly, because he was so interested in looking around at all the other skaters. He admired the way they whizzed in and out and round and round and through and past and out and in and round. He dug his claws lovingly into Arabel's shoulder.

"If I had three skates, Mortimer," said Arabel, "you could sit on the third one and ride. I wish I had."

Mortimer wished it too.

"Tell you what," said Arabel, "I'll take my skates off. I don't feel much like skating."

She sat down at the edge, took her skates off, carried one, and lifted Mortimer on to the other, which she pulled along by the laces.

"Coooo!" shrieked Cindy, whirling past. "Look at scaredy-baby Arabel, pulling her silly old rook along."

"Around the ritzy rink the ragged rookie rumbles," screeched Mindy.

"Scared to skate, scared to skate," chanted Lindy.

They really were horrible girls.

Arabel went very slowly over to where her mother and Auntie Brenda were sitting.

"Can I go home, please Ma?" she said. "My legs ache."

"Oh, go on, ducky, have another try," said Auntie Brenda. "There's nothing to be scared of, really there isn't. You've got to fall down a few times before you learn. It won't hurt you."

But Mrs Jones looked carefully at her daughter and said, "Don't you feel well, dearie?"

"No," said Arabel, and two tears rolled slowly down her cheeks. Mrs Jones put a hand on Arabel's forehead.

"It's hot," she said, "I think we'd better go home, Brenda."

"Oh my goodness," said Auntie Brenda rather crossly. "Can't she stay another half-hour?"

Mrs Jones shook her head. "I don't think she ought."

"Oh, dear. The girls *will* be upset." Brenda raised her voice in a terrific shout. "Cindy! Lindy! Mindy! Come along – your cousin's not feeling well."

Arabel's three cousins came dragging slowly

across the rink with sulky expressions.

"*Now* what?" said Mindy.

"We only just got here," said Cindy.

"Just because 'orrible Arabel can't skate –" said Lindy.

"Ma? Can't you and I go home by bus?" Arabel said.

Auntie Brenda and the three girls looked hopeful at this, but Mrs Jones shook her head again. "I think we ought to get you home as quickly as possible. Besides, I've left my shopping-bag in the boot of your car, Brenda."

"Oh, very well," said Brenda impatiently. "Come on girls."

They took their skates off very slowly and all trailed off to the car park, which was the multi-storey kind. Aunt Brenda's car was up on the fourth level.

Mortimer was very sorry to leave the rink. He looked back disappointedly as long as the skaters were in sight. But when they came within view of the car park he cheered up again.

"It's not worth waiting for the lift," said Auntie Brenda. So they walked up.

Arabel's legs ached worse and worse; Mortimer

and the skates, which she was carrying, seemed heavier and heavier. But Mortimer was even more interested by the car park than he had been by the skating-rink. He gazed round at the huge concrete slopes, and the huge level stretches, and the cars dotted about everywhere, yellow, red, blue, green, black, orange, and silver, like berries on a huge concrete tree.

Mortimer's eyes sparkled like blackcurrant wine gums.

While Auntie Brenda was rummaging for her car key at the bottom of her cluttered handbag, Arabel's arms began to ache so much that she put her skates down on the ground.

With a neat wriggle, Mortimer slid from Arabel's grasp, and climbed on to one of her skates. Then he half spread his wings and gave himself a mighty shove-off. The roller-skate, with Mortimer sitting on it, went whizzing with the speed of a Vampire jet along the flat concrete runway between the two rows of parked cars.

"Oh quick, stop him, stop him!" said Arabel. "He'll go down the ramp."

She meant to shout, but the words only came in a whisper.

Lindy, Mindy, and Cindy rushed after Mortimer. But they bumped into each other, and were too late to catch him. So he shot down the ramp on to the third level.

"Nevermore, nevermore, nevermore, *nevermore!*" he shouted joyfully, and gave himself another shove with his wings, off a parked Citroen, which sent him up the ramp on the opposite side, and back on to the fourth level.

"There he goes – there!" cried Auntie Brenda. "Catch him quickly, girls!" But Cindy, Mindy and Lindy were now out of earshot down on the third level.

"Oh good gracious me did you ever see anything so outrageously provoking in all your born *days*?" said Mrs Jones. "I never did, not even when I worked at the Do-it-yourself delicatessen; don't you go running after that black feathered monster, Arabel, you stay right here."

But Arabel had gone toiling up after Mortimer to the fifth level.

"Mortimer! Please come back!" she pleaded, in her voice that would not come out any louder than a whisper. "*Please* come back. I don't feel very well. I'll bring you here again another day when the wind's not quite so cold."

Mortimer didn't hear her.

Up on the fifth level the wind was icy, and whistled like a saw-blade. Arabel began to shiver and couldn't stop.

Mortimer was having a wonderful time, shooting up and down the ramps, in and out between the cars, rowing himself along with his wings at a terrific rate.

Other people, car-owners, began running after him.

"Stop that bird!" shouted Auntie Brenda, and she added angrily to her sister, "Why you ever

wanted to bring him here I really cannot imagine."

Lots of people were after Mortimer now; but he was going so extremely fast that it was easy for him to dodge them; he had discovered the knack of steering the roller-skate with his tail; he spun round corners and between people's legs and umbrellas and shopping-baskets as if he were entered for the All-Europe Raven Bobsleigh Finals.

After ten minutes there must have been at least fifty people chasing from one ramp to another, all over and up and down the multi-storey car park.

In the end, Mortimer was caught quite by chance when a solidly-built lady, who had just come in from the outside stairs, spread open her umbrella to twirl the rain off before closing it; Mortimer, swinging round a Ford Capri on one wheel, ran full tilt into the umbrella and found himself tangled among the spokes. By the time he was untangled Auntie Brenda, very cross, had marched up and seized him by the scruff.

"*Now* perhaps we can get a move on," she snapped, and carried him kicking back to the car. "He can go in your shopper, Martha," she said grimly, "then he won't be able to give any more trouble. I really don't know why you wanted to come to the roller-skating rink with a *raven*."

Mrs Jones was too anxious about Arabel to argue.

After five minutes or so, Lindy, Cindy and Mindy came panting and straggling back from the fourth level, and Arabel came shivering back from the fifth.

They all climbed into the car.

Chapter Three

As Auntie Brenda drove out of the multi-storey car park, Arabel felt most peculiar. She just couldn't stop shivering.

"Where's Mortimer?" she whispered.

"He's in the boot and there he'll stay till you get home," Auntie Brenda said. "That bird's in disgrace."

Arabel started to say, "He didn't know he was doing anything wrong. He thought the car park was a skating rink for ravens," but the words stuck inside, as if her throat were full of grit.

By the time they reached the Jones's house, Number Six, Rainwater Crescent, Arabel was crying as well as shivering. She couldn't seem to stop doing either of those things.

Mrs Jones jumped out of the car and almost carried Arabel into the house.

"Your shopper!" Brenda shouted after her,

getting the tartan bag out from the boot.

"Put it in the front hall, Brenda."

Brenda did. But she and Martha had exactly similar shopping-bags on wheels, which they had bought together at a grand clearance sale in Rumbury Bargain Basement Bazaar. Brenda put the wrong shopping-bag in the front hall. She left the one that still contained Mortimer in her car boot. Besides Mortimer, it also held two pounds of ripe bananas. Mortimer, who dearly loved bananas and never got nearly enough of them, was too busy just then to complain about being shut inside the bag.

"We'll get home quick," Auntie Brenda said. "We won't hang about in case what Arabel's got is something catching."

She had to make three stops in any case, on the way home, for Cindy wanted a Dairy Isobar, Lindy wanted a Hokey-Coke, and Mindy wanted a bag of Chewy Gooeys; all these things had to be bought at different shops. By the time they reached Auntie Brenda's house, Mortimer had finished the bananas and was willing to be released from the tartan bag.

When Auntie Brenda undid the zip, expecting

to see two raspberry dairy bricks, half a dozen hundred-watt light bulbs, and a head of celery, out shot Mortimer, leaving behind him an utter tangle of empty rinds and squashed banana pulp.

"Oh my dear cats alive!" said Auntie Brenda.

Mortimer was so smothered in banana pulp that for a minute she did not even recognise him. But when she did she cried: "Girls! It's that awful bird of Arabel's. Quick! Catch the nasty brute. He needs teaching a lesson, that bird does."

Lindy snatched up a walking-stick, Cindy got a tennis racket, Mindy found a shrimping-net left over from last summer at Prittlewell-on-Sea. They started chasing Mortimer all over the house.

Mortimer never flew if he could help it; he preferred walking at a dignified pace, or, better still, being pulled along on a truck; but just now it seemed best to fly. He found it slightly difficult to open his wings because of all the mashed banana, but he managed it. He flew to the drawing-room mantelpiece. Mindy took a swipe at him with her shrimping-net and knocked off the gilt clock under its glass dome.

Mortimer left the mantelpiece and flew to the light in the middle of the room; he dangled from it

upside down like a bat, shaking off particles of
banana. Cindy whirled her tennis racket and sent
the light, bulb, shade and all, smashing through
the window. Mortimer had left just before and
flown to the top of the bookshelf. Lindy tried to
hook him with her walking-stick, but all she did
was break a glass pane of the bookshelf door.

"Use your hands, idiot," shouted Auntie Brenda. "You're breaking the place up."

So they dropped their sticks and rackets and nets and went after Mortimer with their hands. Mortimer never, never pecked Arabel. But then she had never pulled his tail, or grabbed him by the leg, or nearly wrenched his wing out of its socket; fairly soon Cindy, Lindy, and Mindy were covered with peck-marks and bleeding quite freely here and there.

Auntie Brenda tried throwing a tablecloth over Mortimer. That didn't catch him; she knocked over a table lamp and a jar of chrysanthemums. But, after a long chase, she managed to get him cornered in the fireplace.

The fire was not lit.

Mortimer went up the chimney.

"Now we've got him," said Auntie Brenda.

"He'll fly out at the top," said Lindy.

"He can't, there's a cowl on it," said Cindy.

They could hear Mortimer scrabbling in the chimney and muttering "Nevermore," to himself.

Auntie Brenda telephoned the sweep, whose name was Ephraim Suckett; she asked him to come round right away.

In ten minutes he arrived, full of curiosity, with his long flexible rods, and his brushes, and his huge vacuum cleaner, which looked like a tar barrel with a tube leading out of it.

"Been having a party?" Mr Suckett said, looking round the drawing-room. "Wonderful larks teenagers get up to."

"We've got a bird in the chimney," said Auntie Brenda. "I want you to get him out as soon as you can."

"A bird, eh?" said Mr Suckett cautiously, looking at the damage. "He wouldn't be one o' them Anacondors with a wing-spread of twenty foot? If so I want extra cover in advance under my Industrial Injuries Policy."

"He's an ordinary common raven," snapped Auntie Brenda. "Please get him out quickly. I want to light the fire. My husband will be home soon."

So Mr Suckett poked one of his rods up the chimney as far as it would go, and then screwed another on to the bottom end and poked that up, and then screwed another one on to *that*. The rods bent like liquorice. A lot of soot fell into the hearth.

"When did you last have this chimney swept?"

Mr Sucket asked. "Coronation year?"

Mortimer retired further up the chimney.

Meanwhile, what had happened to Arabel?

She had gone to hospital.

Mrs Jones rang the doctor as soon as she was indoors. The doctor came quickly and said that Arabel had a nasty case of bronchitis, she would be better off in Rumbury Central, so Mr Jones, who had just come home, drove her there at once in his taxi, wrapped up in three pink blankets with her feet on a hot-water-bottle.

"Where's Mortimer? Is he all right?" whispered Arabel in the taxi. "What about his tea?"

"Father will give him his tea when he gets home after leaving us," said Mrs Jones. Mrs Jones was allowed to stay with Arabel.

She had clean forgotten about Mortimer being inside the tartan shopping-bag.

Mr Jones left his wife and daughter at the hospital, and drove home slowly and sadly. He put his taxi away in its shed. In the front hall he found a tartan shopping-bag containing two raspberry dairy bricks, some light bulbs, and a head of celery. He ate the celery and put the other things away. "Wonder why Martha got all those bulbs?" he thought. "She must know there's a dozen already in the tool cupboard."

Still hungry, even after the celery, he made himself a pot of tea and a large dish of spaghetti in cheese sauce, which was the only thing he knew how to cook.

Then, suddenly, it struck him that the house was unusually quiet. Normally, when Mortimer was about, there would be a scrunching, or a scraping, or a tapping, or a tinkling, as the raven carefully took something to pieces, or knocked something over to see if it would break, or chewed it to see if it was chewable, or pushed one thing underneath some other thing.

"Mortimer?" called Mr Jones. "Where are you? What are you doing? Stop whatever it is, and come here."

No answer. Nobody said "Nevermore." The house remained silent.

Mr Jones began to feel anxious. Although not a man to make a fuss of people, he was fond of Mortimer. Also he wanted to be quite sure the raven was not eating the back wall of the house, or digging a hole under the boiler, or unravelling the bath towels (Mortimer could take a whole bath towel to pieces in three-and-a-half minutes flat, leaving ten miles of snaggled yarn draped over the floor), or munching up the Home Handyman's Encyclopaedia in ten volumes. Or anything else.

High and low, Mr Jones hunted over the whole house for Mortimer, and didn't find him anywhere.

"Oh my dear cats," he thought, "the bird must have wandered out unbeknownst while we were getting Arabel into the taxi with the pink blankets. She will be upset when she hears he's gone. How shall we ever be able to break it to her? She thinks the world of that bird."

Just then the telephone rang.

When Mr Jones lifted the receiver of its rest, words came out of it in a solid shriek.

"What's that?" said Mr Jones, listening. "Who is that? This is Jones's Taxi Service, Rumbury Town. *Brenda?* Is that you? Is something the matter?"

The shriek went on. All Mr Jones could distinguish was something about chrysanthemums, and something about a clock.

"Soot in the clock," he thought, "that's unusual. Maybe they've got an oil-fired clock, I daresay such things do exist, and Brenda's always been dead keen on having everything very up-to-date. I can't help you, Brenda, I'm afraid," he said into the telephone. "I don't know much about oil-fired clocks; matter of fact I don't really know anything at all; you'll have to wait till Arthur gets home. We're all at sixes and sevens here because Arabel's gone to hospital."

And he rang off; he felt he had more things to worry about than soot in his sister-in-law's clock.

Meanwhile, what had been happening to Mortimer?

Mr Suckett the sweep had fastened all his rods together and poked them up Auntie Brenda's chimney. Mortimer had retired right to the very top; but he could not get out. It was possible to see out though through the slits of the cowl, and he found the view very interesting, for the house was right on top of Rumbury Hill. Mortimer could see for miles, over Rumbury Heath, down across London as far as the Houses of Parliament.

Mr Suckett's rods were not quite long enough to dislodge Mortimer; Auntie Brenda's chimney was unusually high.

Discovering this, Mr Suckett began pulling his

rods down again, and unscrewing them one by one.

"What'll you do now?" asked Lindy.

"Will you have to take the top of the chimney off?" asked Mindy.

"Shall we light a fire and toast him?" said Cindy.

"Just get rid of him *somehow* and be quick about it," said Auntie Brenda.

"We'll have to suck him out," said the sweep.

He withdrew the last of his rods, and wheeled his vacuum cleaner close up to the fireplace.

This cleaner was like an ordinary household one, but about eight times larger, with eight times as powerful a suck. It had a big canvas drum on wheels, into which all the soot was sucked down the tube. When he had finished a chimney-sweeping job, Mr Suckett wheeled the drumful of soot away, and sold the soot to people at fifty-nine pence a pound, to put on their slugs. Better than orange-peel, he said it was.

By now the canvas drum was packed to bursting with all the soot that had been in Auntie Brenda's chimney, piling up since Coronation year.

Mr Suckett shoved the nozzle of the long tube right up the chimney and switched on the motor.

It had a tremendously powerful suck. It could yank a St Bernard dog right off its feet and up a ten-foot ramp at an angle of thirty degrees against a force six wind. It sucked Mortimer down the chimney like one of his own feathers.

He shot down backwards, along the canvas tube, and ended up inside the canvas drum, stuffed in with a hundredweight of soot.

Mortimer had quite enjoyed being in the chimney where, if dark, it was interesting, besides there had been that pleasant view from the top.

But he did not at all enjoy being sucked down so fast – backwards and upside-down too – still less did he like being packed into a bag full of suffocating black powder.

He began to kick and flap and peck and shout "Nevermore". In less time than it takes to tell, he had jabbed and clawed a huge hole in the side of the canvas drum; he burst through this hole like a black bombshell, and a hundredweight of soot followed him out.

Auntie Brenda had opened all the windows when Mr Suckett began poking his rods up the

chimney; she said the smell of soot made her faint; Mortimer went out through a window with the speed of a Boeing 707; he had had enough of Auntie Brenda's house.

He left a scene of such blackness and muddle behind him that I do not really think it would be worth trying to describe it.

Chapter Four

Mortimer did not fly very far; he really disapproved of flying. As soon as he was in the street he glided down to the ground and set off walking. He had no idea where Auntie Brenda's house was, nor where Arabel's house was, but this did not worry him. Since Auntie Brenda's house was on the top of a hill he walked downhill, and he studied each front door as he passed it, in case it was the right one. None were. He walked very slowly.

Mr Jones was just going to start eating his spaghetti, and wondering if he should call up the hospital to ask how Arabel was getting on, when the telephone rang.

It was Mrs Jones.

"Is that you, Ben?" she said. "Oh dear, Ben, Arabel's ever so ill, tossing and turning and deliriated, and she keeps asking for Mortimer and the doctor says it will be all right for you to bring him as the sight of him might do her good."

Mr Jones's heart fell into his sheepskin slippers.

"But Mortimer's not here," he said.

"Not *there*? Whatever do you mean, Ben, he must be there?"

Then, for the first time Mrs Jones remembered and let out a guilty gulp. "Oh bless my soul whatever will I forget next? I quite forgot that poor bird, though gracious knows the bother he caused with the coffee beans and the car park and throwing conkers at Ginger who never touched a feather of his tail (not but what he would if he could I daresay). Anyhow a couple of hours shut up in a bag won't have done him any harm but no more than he deserves for all his troublesomeness, anyway you better let him out right away, poor thing."

"Let him out of *where*?"

"My zip tartan shopping-bag. He's inside it."

"No he's not, Martha," said Mr Jones. "There was a head of celery, two family dairy bricks, and half a dozen hundred-watt bulbs. What did you want to get *them* for? There's lots in the tool cupboard."

Mrs Jones let out another squawk. "Oh my

stars, then he must be at Brenda's! She must have left the wrong bag. I hope those girls of hers aren't teasing him. You'd better go right round there and fetch him, Ben, and bring him to the hospital, and bring two more of Arabel's nighties, can you, and a packet of tea-bags and my digestive mint lozenges."

"Round at Brenda's, is he?" Mr Jones said slowly. A lot of things began to make sense to him, the soot and the chrysanthemums and the clock. "All right, Martha, I'll go and fetch him and bring him to you as soon as I can."

He did not mention to Martha about the clock and the chrysanthemums; she had enough to worry about already. He rang off, then dialled Brenda's number.

There was no reply. In fact the line seemed to be out of order; Mr Jones could hear a kind of muffled sound at the other end, but that was all.

It wasn't hard to guess that if there had been any trouble at Brenda's house, then Mortimer the raven was somehow connected with that trouble.

Mr Jones scratched his head. Then he took off his slippers and put on his shoes and overcoat again. Sighing, he drove his taxi out of its shed, turned right, and went up to where Rainwater Crescent meets Rumbury High Street. This is quite a busy junction and there are four traffic lights, or should be; this evening they did not seem to be working.

The traffic was in a horrible tangle. Two policemen were trying to sort it out, and a third was inspecting, with the help of a big torch, the chewed stumps like celery-ends that were all that was left of the Rainwater junction lights.

"Evening, Sid," said Mr Jones, putting his head out of the cab window. "What's up, then?"

"That you, Ben? Well, you'll think I'm barmy, but someone seems to have eaten the traffic lights."

"Oh," said Mr Jones.

He reflected. Then he did a U-turn – luckily there was nobody behind him – and drove down the crescent again. Twenty yards farther down he got out of the cab.

"Mortimer?" he called. "Where are you?"

"Nevermore," said a voice at ankle level in the dark behind him. Although he had been expecting something of the kind, Mr Jones jumped. Then he turned round, and saw Mortimer, with his eyes shining in the light of the street lamps, walking slowly along by the hedge, peering in at all the front gates of the houses as he came to them. He was on the wrong side of the street, so it was likely that he would have passed clean by Number Six and gone on goodness knows where.

Mr Jones picked him up. Mortimer was never a light bird but at the moment, with two pounds of bananas inside him, he weighed as much as the London Telephone Directories with the classified section as well.

"I daresay I ought to hand you over to the police for eating the traffic lights and causing an obstruction," Mr Jones said severely, "but Arabel's ill in hospital so I'm going to take you to see her first, we'll worry about the other things tomorrow. And you'd better behave yourself in the hospital; they won't stand for any tricks there."

"Kaaaark," said Mortimer. Mr Jones was not absolutely encouraged by the way he said it. But there was no time to go into a lot of explanations about hospitals; besides, it was unlikely that Mortimer would listen.

Mr Jones hurried home to pack up the nightdresses, teabags, and digestive peppermint lozenges. While he was doing this, Mortimer wandered into the kitchen and saw the large dish of spaghetti that Mr Jones had cooked for his supper.

"Nevermore," he said sadly. He walked all round the dish, studying it from every side.

Mortimer loved spaghetti in cheese sauce, it was one of his favourite between-meals snacks, but just at the moment he was so full of bananas that he found himself unable to eat a single string.

Even if he couldn't eat the spaghetti, though, he didn't want to let it go to waste. He looked for a box, jar, or container to put it in; when allowed to do so, Mortimer would stay happy and busy for quite a long time, packing spaghetti into yoghourt pots or egg boxes or whatever happened to be at hand.

He had just tidied away the last of the spaghetti when Mr Jones hurried back with the mints and nightdresses, grabbed a box of teabags from the kitchen cupboard, dropped all these things into the tartan zip bag, put on his overcoat again, and picked up Mortimer.

He did not notice that the spaghetti dish was empty.

By now it was quite late at night, but Mr Jones supposed that it would be all right to go to the hospital, even though it was after visiting hours, since the doctor had told him to bring Mortimer.

He drove his taxi to Rumbury Central, parked in the big front forecourt, and walked inside with Mortimer on his shoulder.

Mortimer was amazed by the hospital. He liked it even better than the multi-storey car park. It had been built about a hundred years ago by Florence Nightingale, of black-pudding coloured brick. It was huge, like a prison; several of its corridors were about a mile long. The ceilings were so high that the echoes from the smallest sound, even sounds out in the street, were as loud as thunder. Many patients believed that nurses and doctors were allowed to drive cars along the corridors, but this was not actually the case.

Mr Jones went up to the fourth floor in a great creaking lift as big as a post office. Mortimer said "Kaark," because the lift reminded him of Rumbury Town Station. They walked along miles of green-floored passage until they found Balaclava Ward.

When they reached the door there was nobody

in sight to tell Mr Jones whether he was allowed to go in. But there were two large windows like portholes in the doors, so Mr Jones stood on tiptoe, with Mortimer on his shoulder, and peered through.

He could see a double row of white-covered beds, six on each side, and half-way along, his wife Martha, sitting by one of them. He caught her eye and waved; she made signs that he was to wait until the Sister – who wore a white pie-frill cap and sat at a desk near the door – noticed him and let him in.

Mr Jones nodded to show he understood.

He stuck his hands in his pockets and prepared to wait quietly.

But he didn't wait quietly. Instead he let out a series of such piercing yells that patients shot bolt upright in their beds all over that part of the hospital, porters rammed their trolleys into doors, nurses dropped whole trays of instruments, and doctors swallowed the ends of their stethoscopes.

Mortimer, who had been sitting very quiet and interested, looking about him, flew straight up in the air and circled round and round, flapping his wings and shouting, "Nevermore, *nevermore*!"

Mr Jones fainted dead away on the floor.

Sister Bridget Hagerty came rushing out of the ward. She was small and black-haired and freckled; her eyes were as blue as blue scouring-powder; when she gave orders for a thing to be done, it was done right away. But everybody liked her.

"What in the name of goodness is going on here?" she snapped.

Dr Antonio arrived. He was in charge of that part of the hospital at night; he had just come on duty. He was not the doctor who had told Mrs Jones to have Mortimer brought along; in fact Dr Antonio could not stand birds. He had been frightened by a tame cockatoo at the age of three, in his pram; ever since then, the sight of any bird larger than a bluetit brought him out in a rash.

He came out in a rash now, bright scarlet, at the sight of Mortimer.

"It's obvious what's going on!" he said. "That great black brute has attacked this poor fellow. Palgrave! Where are you? Come here, quick!"

Palgrave was the ward orderly. He had gone off to fetch the doctor a cup of instant coffee. He came running along the corridor.

"Palgrave, get that bird out of here, quickly!"

"Yes sir, right away, sir," said Palgrave, and he opened the landing window and threw the cup of hot coffee all over Mortimer, who was still circling round up above, wondering what was the matter with Mr Jones.

Mortimer didn't care for coffee unless it was very sweet, and his feelings were hurt; he flew straight out of the window.

"Doctor, there's something very funny about this man," said Sister Bridget, who was kneeling down by Mr Jones. "Why do you suppose his hands are all covered with spaghetti in cheese sauce?"

"Perhaps he's a burn case, an emergency," suggested the doctor. "Perhaps he couldn't find anything else and so he used the spaghetti as a burn dressing. We had better take him along to Casualty. Palgrave, get a stretcher."

"But his pockets are full of spaghetti too," said Sister Bridget.

"Perhaps he was on his way to meet some Italian friends," said the doctor. "Perhaps he *is* Italian. Parla Italiano?" he shouted hopefully into Mr Jones's ear.

Mr Jones groaned.

"Parla Italiano?" said the doctor again.

Mr Jones, who had flown over Italy as a pilot in World War II, said feebly, "Have we crashed? Where's my rear gunner? Where's my navigator?"

"A mental case," said Dr Antonio. "Speaks English, hands covered in spaghetti, asks for his navigator; without doubt, a mental case. Palgrave, fetch a straight-jacket."

Palgrave put down the stretcher he had just brought and went off again.

Luckily at this moment Mrs Jones came out of Balaclava Ward, wondering what was going on, and what had become of Ben. When she saw him lying on the ground, his hands covered in spaghetti, she let out a gasp.

"Oh, Ben, dear! What ever has been happening?"

"Do you know this man, Mrs Jones?" asked Sister Bridget.

"It's my husband! What's happened?"

"He seems to have fainted," said the Sister.

Mr Jones came to a bit more. "Is that you, Martha?" he said faintly. "Worms. Worms in my pocket. It was the shock –"

"Oh my goodness gracious I should think so, whatever next?" cried his wife. "Worms in your pocket, how did they come to be there, then?"

"It wasn't worms, it was spaghetti," said Sister Bridget, helping Mr Jones to sit up and fanning him with the straight-jacket Palgrave had brought. "Could you fetch a cup of tea, please, Palgrave? How did you come to have your pockets full of spaghetti, Mr Jones?"

"Instant coffee, instant stretcher, instant straight-jacket, instant tea," grumbled Palgrave, stomping off again.

"Spaghetti? Oh, that must have been Mortimer, it's just like his naughty ways," said Mrs Jones. "Last time I left him alone with a bowl of spaghetti for five minutes he packed the whole bowlful in among my Shetland knitting wool. Arabel's friends were asking where she got her spaghetti-Fair Isle sweater for weeks after. *Ben!* Where *is* Mortimer?"

Mr Jones struggled to his feet and drank the cup of tea Palgrave had just brought.

"Mortimer? Isn't he here? He was here just now. Have you seen a raven?" he asked Palgrave.

"Raven? Big black hairy bird? I chucked him out the window with a cup of Whizzcaff over his tail feathers," said Palgrave. "Doc told me to."

"Oh, no!" wailed Mrs Jones. "Dr Plantaganet said the medicine didn't seem to be having any effect and a sight of Mortimer was the one thing that might make Arabel feel better."

She looked beseechingly at the Sister. Sister Bridget looked at Palgrave. Palgrave looked at the doctor, who looked at his feet.

"Better go outside and start hunting for him, and quick about it," said the Sister.

"Instant coffee, instant strait-jacket, instant tea, instant raven," grumbled Palgrave, and followed the doctor out through the fire door on to the fire escape. It was raining hard, and very dark indeed.

Chapter Five

Where, all this time, *was* Mortimer?

Outside the windows of Balaclava Ward there was a balcony that ran right round the building. Mortimer, when urged out of the window so rudely, had flown no farther than the balcony parapet. There he sat in the dark, thinking gloomy thoughts.

He was tired. It had been a long, exciting day: first of all the roller-skating, then the bananas, then the chimney, then the soot, then the two-mile walk from Auntie Brenda's house to Rainwater Cresent. Then the traffic lights.

Mortimer's feet were sore and his tail feathers felt fitgety from the Whizzcaff, he was all sooty, and his wings ached where Lindy, Mindy, and Cindy had pulled them, and he wanted to go to sleep. He longed for his lovely cosy shiny white enamel bread bin.

But he also had a feeling that Arabel was not far away, and he wanted to see her.

He was not happy about her.

Limping a little, muttering and croaking under his breath, he began to side along the parapet of the balcony, looking through each window in turn as he came to it.

Just inside the third window there stood a bed which at first sight looked as if it had no patient in it; the person was so very small, and lying so very flat, and not moving at all.

Mortimer flapped across from the parapet to the window-sill, and looked through the glass, his black eyes as bright and sharp as pencil points.

"Kaaaark!" he said.

The person in the bed didn't stir.

Mortimer tapped on the closed window with his beak.

Nobody came to let him in. Sister Bridget was talking quietly to Mr and Mrs Jones at the far end of the room. All the other patients were asleep. Nobody heard Mortimer.

Down below, in the pouring rain, Dr Antonio and Palgrave, equipped with torches and butterfly nets, were hunting for Mortimer in the hospital garden. They weren't finding him.

Mortimer sighed. Then he spread his wings and hoisted himself into the air. He flew along the row of windows tapping each in turn. They were all shut. Little ventilators let fresh air into the ward; they were no use to Mortimer.

When he had been all along one side of the ward, and back along the other side, Mortimer flew heavily up over the roof. Here he found a chimney. He perched on it.

The chimney had a familiar sooty smell. Mortimer put his head down inside and listened. Then he sniffed. Then he listened again. Then he tapped his beak against the chimney pot. Then he came to a quick decision and dived head-first down the chimney.

Luckily for Mortimer they had given up using stoves to heat Rumbury Central hospital. Instead they had electric radiators. But the stoves were still there, because no one had time to remove them, and it would make a lot of mess, anyway.

In the middle of Balaclava Ward there stood a big, blue coal-stove, shiny, with a black stove-pipe leading up from it, and two doors that opened in front. They had shiny little mica panes, so that when they were shut you could see the fire behind them, when it was lit.

Mortimer came clattering down the chimney head-first and landed inside the stove (which surprised him very much; it was not what he had expected) with two pounds of clinker and a handful of soot – not nearly so much as had been in Auntie Brenda's chimney because this one had been regularly swept.

He made the most amazing noise inside the

stove. Several of the patients woke up and thought it must be Santa Claus.

Sister Bridget came running.

Mortimer was trying to get the doors open, but he couldn't. He did push his head out through one of the mica panes, though, and glared at Sister Bridget as she came towards him.

"Is this your raven?" Sister Bridget asked Mrs Jones.

"Oh good gracious, bless my precious soul *yes*, however did he get in there, the naughty wretch, I'm sure I don't know, oh, dear, Sister Bridget, do get him out of there quick, please! I'm so anxious about Arabel, she doesn't seem to take notice of *anything*."

Sister Bridget undid the screw that kept the stove doors shut. When she opened the doors, out swung Mortimer, with his head still stuck through one of the panes. Sister Bridget grabbed him round his middle. She didn't hurt him, but she held him tight while she worked his head backwards through the hole he had made.

Then she held him up and had a look at him.

I *never*, in all my born days, saw a bird in such a filthy state!" she said. "That bird is going to have a bath before he goes anywhere near your daughter, Mrs Jones, or my name's not Moira Bridget Hagerty."

"Oh, please be quick then," sobbed Mrs Jones, "for I think he's her only hope, I truly do; oh my goodness I'm sorry I ever said a word against his pecking away the front steps or even munching that hole in the telly and if Arabel gets better he can undo every bathtowel in the house and welcome!"

Sister Bridget carried Mortimer into a white-tiled room called the sluice, and there she suddenly put him under a jet of warm water and squirted liquid soap at him too. Mortimer let out a yell. He struggled as if he were being barbecued. But Sister Bridget took no notice at all. She held him in the jet of water until every speckle of soot had been washed off him. Then she clapped a hair-dryer over him which was so powerful that before you could whistle God Save the Queen he was bone-dry and his feathers were sticking out all round like a dandelion clock.

He was still as black as ever. And by this time he was in a bad temper.

When Sister Bridget lifted the dryer off him he

sidled towards her as if he intended to peck her.

But Sister Bridget stood no nonsense, from nurses, doctors, or ravens.

"Behave yourself, now!" she said sharply to Mortimer, and she picked him up round his black middle again, and put him on Arabel's bedside locker.

"Arabel, dearie," said Mrs Jones. "Here's Mortimer come to see how you're getting on."

Arabel didn't answer. She lay very white and quiet, with her eyes shut. Every now and then she coughed a little. That was all.

Mr Jones gave a gulp and blew his nose.

Mortimer looked at Arabel. He looked at her for a long, long time. He sat still on the polished wooden locker staring at her. Arabel didn't move. Mortimer didn't move either. But two tears ran down, one on either side of his bill.

Then he hopped down on to Arabel's pillow.

He hopped close behind her head, and listened at her left ear. Then he went round to her other side and listened at her right ear.

Then he croaked a little, gently, to himself, and made a tiny scratching noise with his claws on the pillow. Then he waited.

There was a pause. Then, very slowly, Arabel rolled over on to her stomach. She turned her face a little and opened one eye, so that she could just see Mortimer with it.

"Hello, Mortimer," she whispered.

Nobody breathed much.

Then Arabel turned her head the other way, so that she could see Mrs Jones.

"Mortimer's tired. He wants his bread bin," she whispered. "He's very tired."

"Oh, Ben – *quick*!" Mrs Jones said.

Mr Jones went very quickly and quietly out of the ward. He didn't like to run till he was on the other side of the door. Then he fairly hurled himself down the stairs and out through the main entrance to his taxi.

He noticed Palgrave and Dr Antonio, standing in the forecourt, scratching their heads.

"Bird's found – going to get bread bin," Mr Jones panted as he ran by. He drove home as fast as he dared and ran into the kitchen of Number Six, Rainwater Crescent. He tipped one farmhouse, one wholemeal, one currant malt, and a bag of rice buns onto the floor, picked up the bin, and carried it out to the taxi. He hadn't even switched off the engine.

When he got back to the hospital, everybody seemed to be in exactly the same position as when he had left, except that Palgrave was there too, with a pot of cocoa, and Dr Antonio with a bright scarlet rash.

Arabel had shut her eye again, but when her father said, "Here's the bread bin, dearie," she opened it.

"Please put it on the bed," she whispered, and curled herself into a C-shape.

Mr Jones put the bread bin into the middle of the C. It had two enamel handles, one on each side. Mortimer stepped down from Arabel's pillow and climbed carefully, by means of one of the handles, on to the rim of the bin. He perched there for a minute, then he jumped down inside. Then he stuck his head under his wing and went to sleep.

Arabel reached out a hand from under the bedclothes and took hold of the enamel handle. Then, holding the handle, she too went to sleep, quietly and peacefully.

"Would you credit it, now?" said Sister Bridget.

Mr Jones sat down by Mrs Jones and they went on sitting by Arabel all night.

Sister Bridget took Dr Antonio away to put something on his rash.

Palgrave drank up the pot of cocoa himself, as nobody else seemed to want it.

In the morning Dr Plantaganet came to look at Arabel. Her cheeks were just faintly pink, and her eyes were quite bright.

Mortimer was as black as ever, still asleep, with his head under his wing.

"She'll do now," Dr Plantaganet said. "But don't let her out in the rain for a long time."

"She'll have to stay indoors then," said Mrs Jones. "For I don't believe it's ever going to stop raining."

But just then it did stop, and a watery, faint

blink of sun peered through the hospital window. Arabel was too weak to talk still, but she pointed to it and smiled.

Mr Jones leaned over and gave his daughter a kiss, then he went off to drive his taxi and buy a new coal scuttle.

Mrs Jones settled down with her knitting at Arabel's bed.

Mortimer went on sleeping in the bread bin with his head tucked under his wing.

Barn Owl Books

THE PUBLISHING HOUSE DEVOTED ENTIRELY TO
THE REPRINTING OF CHILDREN'S BOOKS

RECENT TITLES

Arabel's Raven – Joan Aiken

Mortimer the raven finds the Joneses and causes chaos in Rumbury Town

The Spiral Stair – Joan Aiken

Giraffe thieves are about! Arabel and her raven have to act fast

Your Guess is as Good as Mine – Bernard Ashley

Nicky gets into a stranger's car by mistake

The Gathering – Isobelle Carmody

Four young people and a ghost battle with a strange evil force

Voyage – Adèle Geras

Story of four young Russians sailing to the U.S. in 1904

Private – Keep Out! – Gwen Grant

Diary of the youngest of six in the 1940s

Leila's Magical Monster Party – Ann Jungman

Leila invites all the baddies to her party and they come!

The Silver Crown – Robert O'Brien
A rare birthday present leads to an extraordinary quest

Playing Beatie Bow – Ruth Park
Exciting Australian time travel story in which Abigail learns about love

The Mustang Machine – Chris Powling
A magic bike sorts out the bullies

The Phantom Carwash – Chris Powling
When Lenny asks for a carwash for Christmas, he doesn't expect to get one, never mind a magic one.

The Intergalactic Kitchen – Frank Rodgers
The Bird family plus their kitchen go into outer space

You're Thinking about Doughnuts – Michael Rosen
Frank is left alone in a scary museum at night

Jimmy Jelly – Jacqueline Wilson
A T.V. personality is confronted by his greatest fan

The Devil's Arithmetic – Jane Yolen
Hannah from New York time travels to Auschwitz in 1942 and acquires wisdom